The Nine Forms of Durga Maa

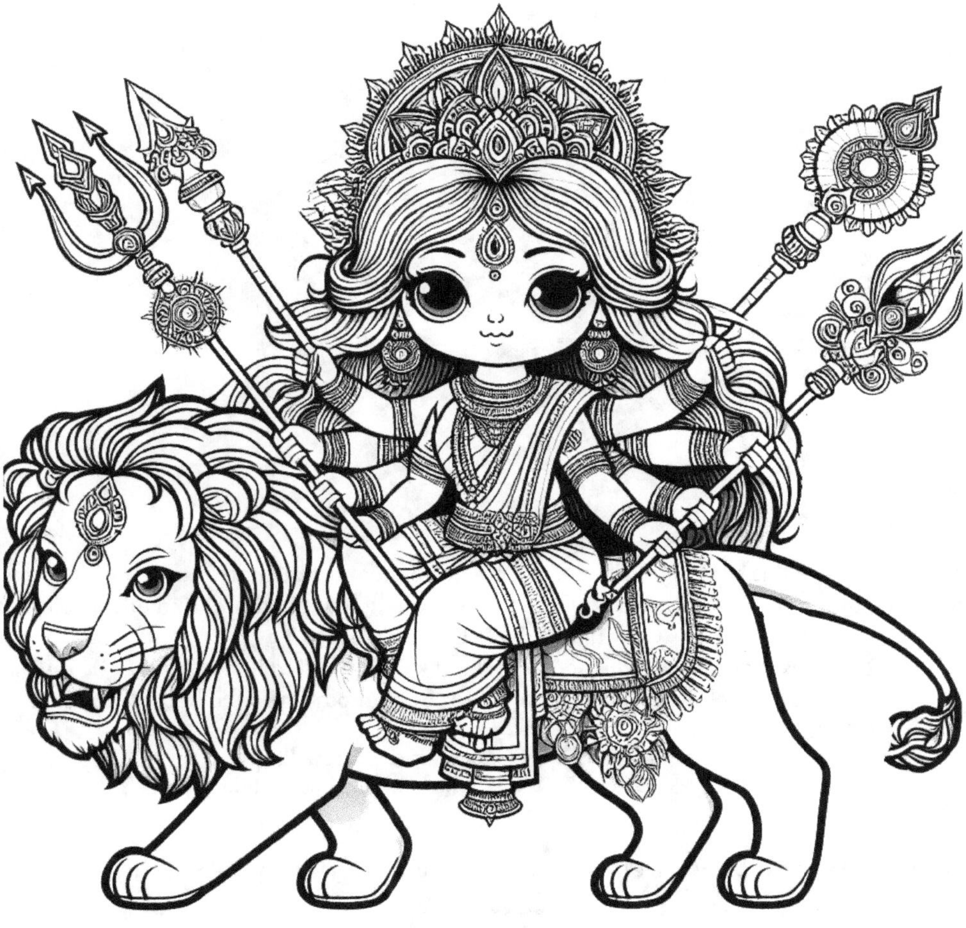

Written By:

Roma Devi Singh

Om Jayanti Mangala Kali Bhadrakali Kapalini,
Durga Kshama Shiva Dhatri, Swaha Swadha Namostute

We invite you to explore other books in the Divine Colors Series and kindly leave a 5-star review if you enjoyed them!

Om Aim Hrim Klim Chamundayai Vicche
To the fierce and loving Goddess Durga Maa,
Your strength guides our family every day.
This book is for you, with love from my heart,
May you always protect us.
To my Mom, Dad , Four Brothers and Family,
Thank you for always believing in me.

Ya Devi Sarvabhuteshu Maa Shailaputri Rupena Samsthita
Namastasyai Namastasyai Namastasyai Namo Namah

Shailaputri Maa, O mountain queen,
In your strength, all is serene.
Riding high on Nandi's might,
Guide us through both day and night.
With your grace, we start this way,
Bless our hearts on this first day.

Shailaputri Maa

SHAILAPUTRI MAA
THE DAUGHTER OF THE MOUNTAIN

SYMBOLISM: SHAILAPUTRI MAA IS THE PUREST FORM OF DURGA, REPRESENTING MOTHER NATURE IN ALL HER GRANDEUR. HER NAME MEANS "DAUGHTER OF THE MOUNTAINS," AS SHE WAS BORN TO THE KING OF THE HIMALAYAS. SHE IS A POWERFUL SYMBOL OF STRENGTH AND STABILITY.

ICONOGRAPHY: SHAILAPUTRI MAA IS DEPICTED RIDING A BULL (NANDI), A SYMBOL OF PEACE AND DETERMINATION. SHE HOLDS A TRIDENT (TRISHUL) IN ONE HAND AND A LOTUS IN THE OTHER, SYMBOLIZING THE BALANCE BETWEEN ACTION AND SPIRITUALITY. HER CALM FACE EXUDES MOTHERLY COMPASSION, AND HER PRESENCE SIGNIFIES GROUNDING AND STABILITY IN LIFE.

SIGNIFICANCE: AS THE FIRST FORM OF DURGA MAA, SHE IS THE EMBODIMENT OF EARTHLY POWER, REPRESENTING A NEW BEGINNING FOR ALL LIVING BEINGS. WORSHIPPING SHAILAPUTRI MAA INVOKES STRENGTH AND THE COURAGE TO START AFRESH.

COLOR: RED

HELP NANDI FIND THE FIELD OF FLOWERS

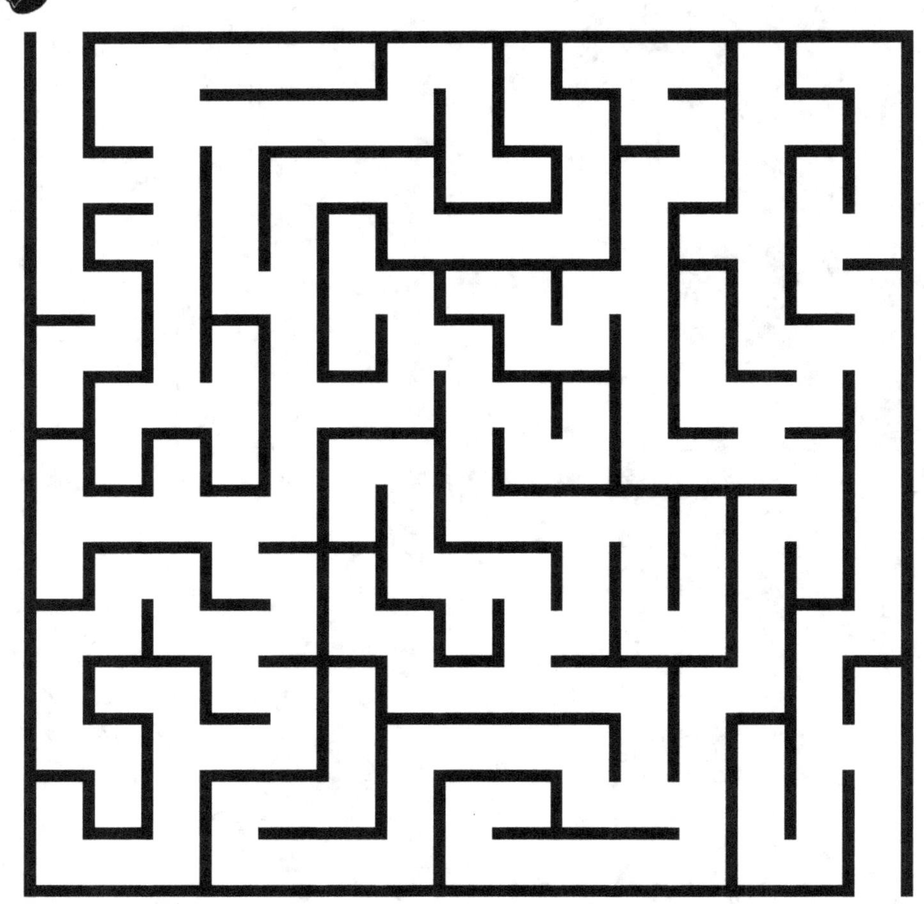

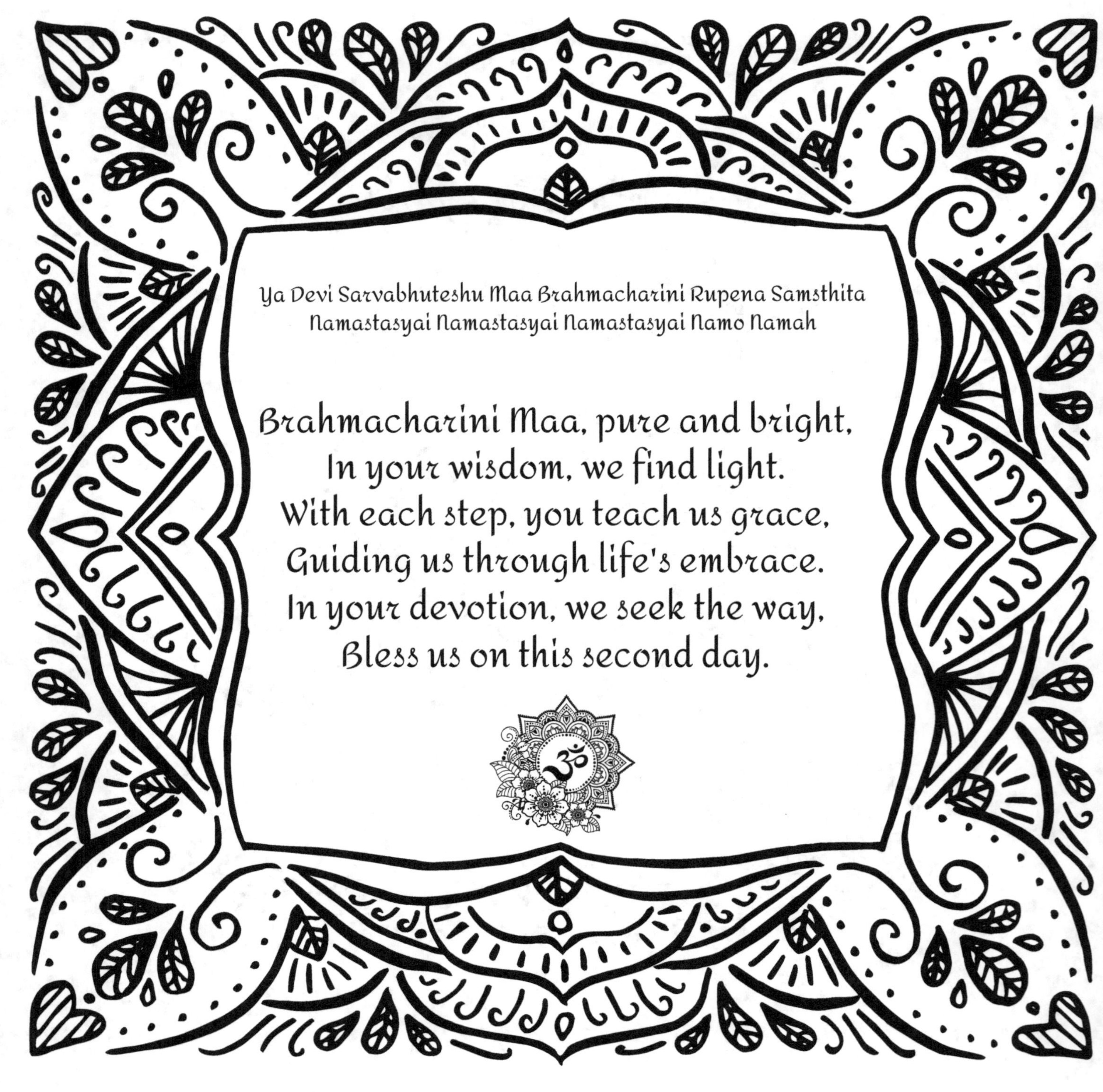

Ya Devi Sarvabhuteshu Maa Brahmacharini Rupena Samsthita
Namastasyai Namastasyai Namastasyai Namo Namah

Brahmacharini Maa, pure and bright,
In your wisdom, we find light.
With each step, you teach us grace,
Guiding us through life's embrace.
In your devotion, we seek the way,
Bless us on this second day.

Brahmacharini Maa

BRAHMACHARINI MAA
THE ASCETIC GODDESS

SYMBOLISM: BRAHMACHARINI MAA REPRESENTS DEVOTION, PENANCE, AND RIGHTEOUSNESS. SHE IS DEPICTED AS A DEVOTED ASCETIC, SYMBOLIZING THE POWER OF SPIRITUAL PRACTICE AND PENANCE IN ACHIEVING INNER PEACE AND SELF-CONTROL.

ICONOGRAPHY: SHE IS SEEN WALKING BAREFOOT WITH A RUDRAKSHA MALA (ROSARY) IN ONE HAND AND A KAMANDALU (WATER POT) IN THE OTHER, SYMBOLIZING HER DEEP CONNECTION TO SPIRITUAL AUSTERITY AND MEDITATION. HER SERENE, CALM DEMEANOR REPRESENTS THE PROFOUND INNER STRENGTH THAT COMES FROM DEDICATION AND WILLPOWER.

SIGNIFICANCE: BRAHMACHARINI MAA IS REVERED FOR HER EMBODIMENT OF DEVOTION AND WISDOM. SHE SIGNIFIES THE IMPORTANCE OF STRONG WILL, PURITY, AND DISCIPLINE, REMINDING DEVOTEES TO REMAIN STEADFAST IN THEIR PURSUITS, NO MATTER HOW CHALLENGING.

COLOR: YELLOW

CONNECT THE DOTS

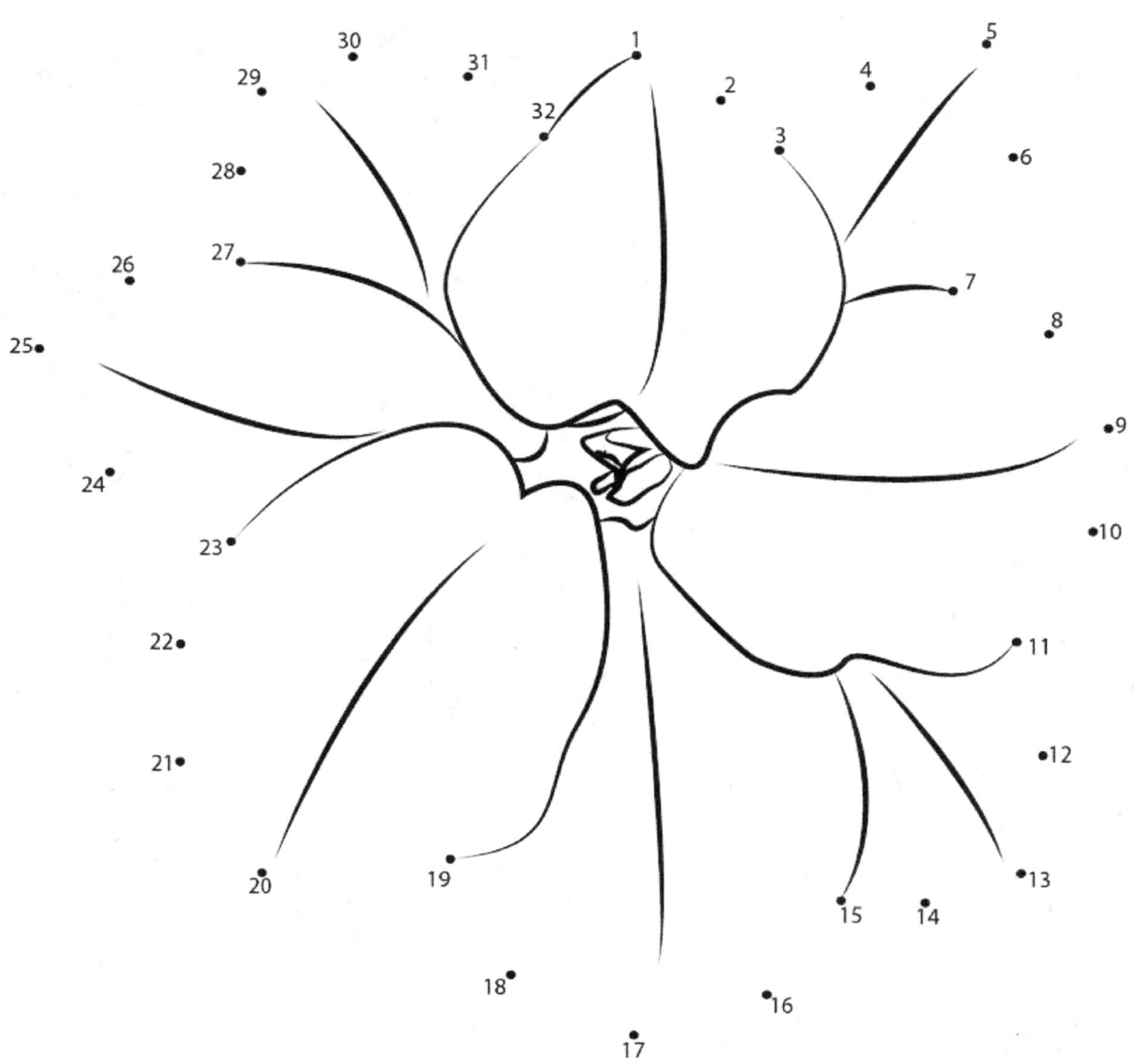

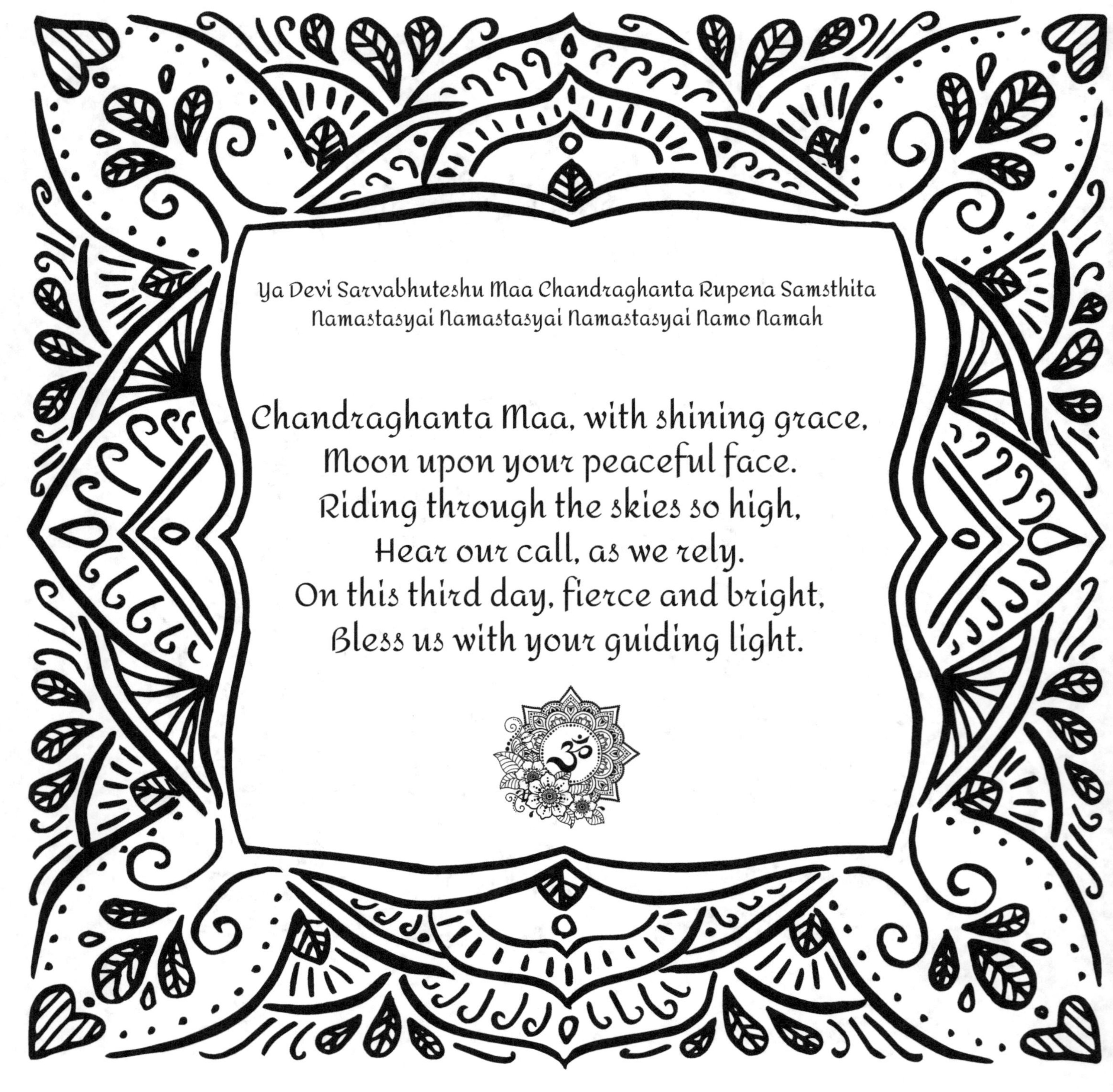

Ya Devi Sarvabhuteshu Maa Chandraghanta Rupena Samsthita
Namastasyai Namastasyai Namastasyai Namo Namah

Chandraghanta Maa, with shining grace,
Moon upon your peaceful face.
Riding through the skies so high,
Hear our call, as we rely.
On this third day, fierce and bright,
Bless us with your guiding light.

Chandraghanta Maa

CHANDRAGHANTA MAA
THE WARRIOR GODDESS WITH A CRESCENT MOON

SYMBOLISM: CHANDRAGHANTA MAA EMBODIES FIERCE STRENGTH, COURAGE, AND PROTECTION. HER NAME COMES FROM THE CRESCENT MOON (CHANDRA) ON HER FOREHEAD, WHICH SYMBOLIZES MENTAL CLARITY, CALM, AND RESILIENCE.

ICONOGRAPHY: SHE IS DEPICTED RIDING A TIGER, THE SYMBOL OF BRAVERY, AND HAS TEN ARMS HOLDING VARIOUS WEAPONS LIKE A MACE, BOW, SWORD, AND TRIDENT. THIS PORTRAYAL HIGHLIGHTS HER READINESS FOR WAR AGAINST THE FORCES OF EVIL. SHE IS ADORNED WITH A CRESCENT MOON ON HER FOREHEAD, GIVING HER THE POWER TO REMOVE ALL OBSTACLES AND FEAR. DESPITE HER FIERCE STANCE, HER FACE EXUDES TRANQUILITY, REFLECTING THE HARMONY BETWEEN COURAGE AND CALMNESS.

SIGNIFICANCE: WORSHIPPING CHANDRAGHANTA MAA BRINGS FEARLESSNESS AND PROTECTION. SHE EMPOWERS DEVOTEES TO FACE CHALLENGES HEAD-ON WITH A BALANCE OF MENTAL PEACE AND ASSERTIVE STRENGTH, SYMBOLIZING THE DESTRUCTION OF INNER AND OUTER DEMONS.

COLOR: WHITE

Chandraghanta Maa
Word Search

M	E	R	G	P	W	Z	P	P	I	J	B
O	P	K	R	U	E	N	E	R	G	Y	E
O	U	O	O	R	N	G	E	U	A	R	L
N	R	F	W	I	G	O	T	M	P	X	L
T	I	T	T	D	E	V	O	T	I	O	N
A	T	Y	H	Y	G	S	H	A	K	T	I
I	Y	S	T	A	B	I	L	I	T	Y	L
N	B	R	O	T	H	E	R	I	G	L	F
S	T	R	E	N	G	T	H	D	D	K	U
T	H	I	R	D	E	Y	E	E	E	Q	V
T	B	I	G	E	I	G	L	O	R	Y	E
B	R	A	V	E	R	Y	A	S	E	S	S

SHAKTI	MOON	ENERGY	BRAVERY
BELL	GLORY	STABILITY	DEVOTION
THIRD EYE	STRENGTH	PURITY	GROWTH

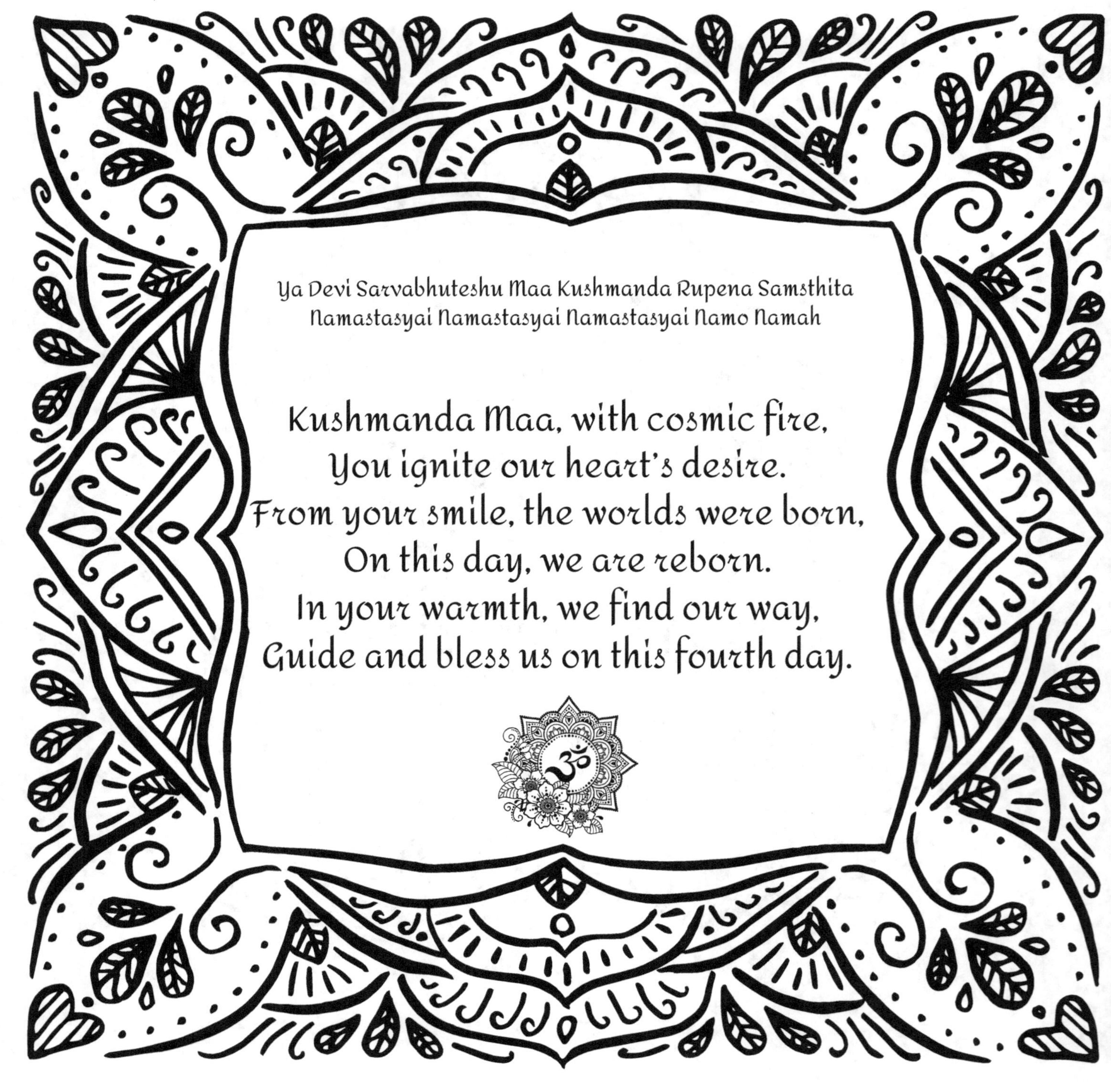

Ya Devi Sarvabhuteshu Maa Kushmanda Rupena Samsthita
Namastasyai Namastasyai Namastasyai Namo Namah

Kushmanda Maa, with cosmic fire,
You ignite our heart's desire.
From your smile, the worlds were born,
On this day, we are reborn.
In your warmth, we find our way,
Guide and bless us on this fourth day.

Kushmanda Maa

KUSHMANDA MAA
THE COSMIC CREATOR

SYMBOLISM: KUSHMANDA MAA REPRESENTS THE COSMIC ENERGY THAT GAVE BIRTH TO THE UNIVERSE. HER NAME, "KU" MEANING LITTLE, "USHMA" MEANING WARMTH, AND "ANDA" MEANING EGG, SIGNIFIES THAT SHE CREATED THE UNIVERSE AS A SMALL COSMIC EGG THROUGH HER RADIANT SMILE.

ICONOGRAPHY: SHE IS DEPICTED WITH EIGHT ARMS, HOLDING DIVINE OBJECTS LIKE A CHAKRA (DISCUS), GADHA (MACE), BOW, LOTUS, AND A KAMANDALU. SHE RIDES A LION, SHOWCASING HER AUTHORITY AND POWER OVER THE COSMOS. HER BODY RADIATES A GLOWING AURA, SIGNIFYING THAT SHE IS THE SUN AT THE CORE OF CREATION, BRINGING WARMTH AND LIGHT TO THE UNIVERSE.

SIGNIFICANCE: WORSHIPPING KUSHMANDA MAA IS BELIEVED TO IMPROVE HEALTH, VITALITY, AND SUCCESS. SHE BESTOWS LIGHT, ENERGY, AND THE POWER TO CREATE NEW BEGINNINGS. HER FORM SYMBOLIZES THE EMERGENCE OF LIFE FROM THE VOID, AND SHE IS ASSOCIATED WITH WEALTH AND WELL-BEING.

COLOR: GREEN

COSMIC HIDDEN WORDS

FIND THE HIDDEN WORDS IN THE SOLAR SYSTEM

Galaxy	Planet	Sun
Mercury	Venus	Saturn
Mars	Star	Neptune

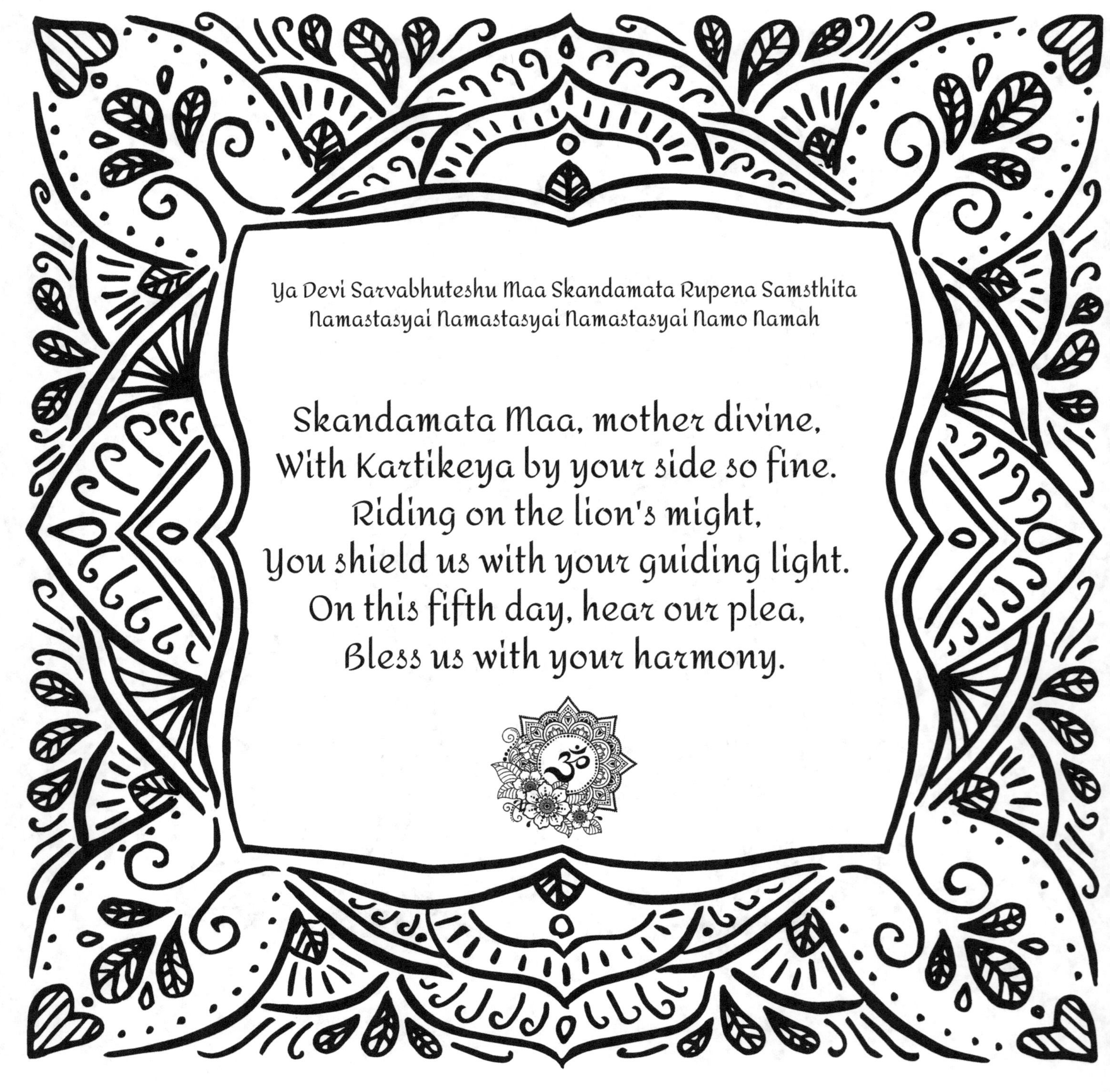

Ya Devi Sarvabhuteshu Maa Skandamata Rupena Samsthita
Namastasyai Namastasyai Namastasyai Namo Namah

Skandamata Maa, mother divine,
With Kartikeya by your side so fine.
Riding on the lion's might,
You shield us with your guiding light.
On this fifth day, hear our plea,
Bless us with your harmony.

Skandamata Maa

SKANDAMATA MAA
THE MOTHER OF LORD SKANDA (KARTIKEYA)

SYMBOLISM: SKANDAMATA MAA IS THE GODDESS OF MOTHERHOOD, REPRESENTING NURTURING, STRENGTH, AND PROTECTIVE LOVE. AS THE MOTHER OF SKANDA (ALSO KNOWN AS KARTIKEYA), THE GOD OF WAR, SHE EPITOMIZES THE BOND BETWEEN MOTHER AND CHILD, AND HER POWER TO PROTECT HER OFFSPRING FROM HARM.

ICONOGRAPHY: SHE IS DEPICTED SEATED ON A LION, CARRYING HER INFANT SON SKANDA IN HER LAP. HER FOUR ARMS HOLD LOTUSES, AND SHE IS SEEN IN A CALM, PROTECTIVE POSTURE. DESPITE BEING A FIERCE WARRIOR MOTHER, HER DEMEANOR RADIATES COMPASSION AND MOTHERLY CARE.

SIGNIFICANCE: SKANDAMATA MAA BLESSES HER DEVOTEES WITH MATERNAL PROTECTION AND PROSPERITY. SHE ALSO REPRESENTS THE DIVINE BALANCE OF NURTURING LOVE AND POWERFUL STRENGTH, REMINDING US OF THE INHERENT STRENGTH IN MOTHERHOOD.

COLOR: BLUE

SKANDA'S CRADLE

DECORATE A CRADLE FOR BABY SKANDA.

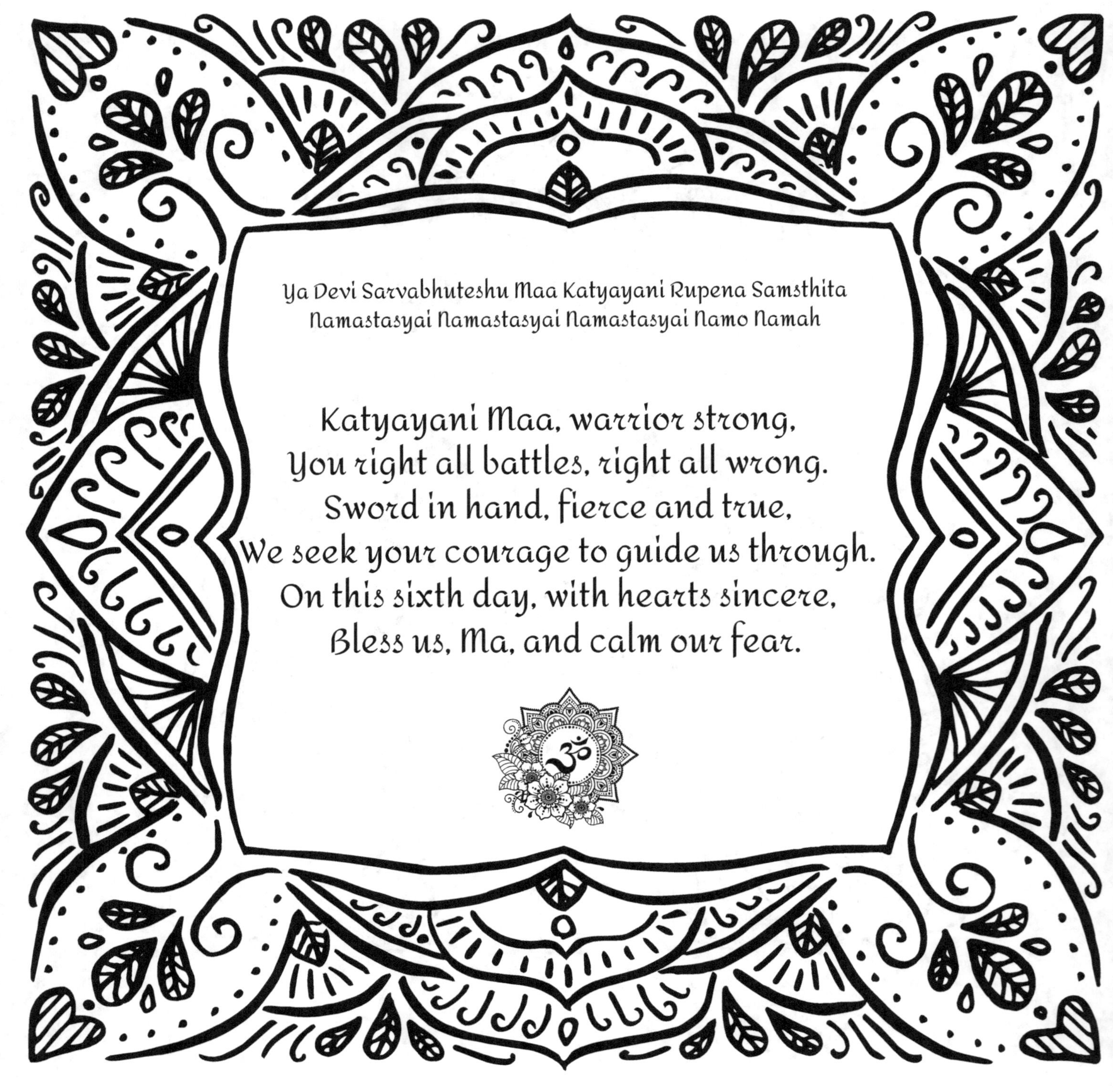

Ya Devi Sarvabhuteshu Maa Katyayani Rupena Samsthita
Namastasyai Namastasyai Namastasyai Namo Namah

Katyayani Maa, warrior strong,
You right all battles, right all wrong.
Sword in hand, fierce and true,
We seek your courage to guide us through.
On this sixth day, with hearts sincere,
Bless us, Ma, and calm our fear.

Katyayani Maa

KATYAYANI MAA
THE WARRIOR GODDESS

SYMBOLISM: KATYAYANI MAA IS A FIERCE WARRIOR GODDESS KNOWN FOR HER POWER TO DESTROY EVIL AND PROTECT THE RIGHTEOUS. SHE IS OFTEN INVOKED FOR STRENGTH, COURAGE, AND VICTORY OVER DARKNESS.

ICONOGRAPHY: SHE IS PORTRAYED RIDING A LION, WITH FOUR ARMS HOLDING A SWORD, SHIELD, AND LOTUS. HER POWERFUL STANCE SIGNIFIES THE BATTLE-READY ATTITUDE OF THE DIVINE MOTHER WHO DESTROYS ALL OBSTACLES. HER NAME ORIGINATES FROM SAGE KATYA, WHO WORSHIPPED DURGA TO BLESS HIM WITH A DAUGHTER. SHE WAS BORN AS KATYAYANI MAA TO DEFEAT THE DEMON MAHISHASURA.

SIGNIFICANCE: KATYAYANI MAA REPRESENTS THE VICTORY OF GOOD OVER EVIL AND IS OFTEN ASSOCIATED WITH THE FULFILLMENT OF DESIRES, PARTICULARLY RELATED TO MARRIAGE AND RELATIONSHIPS. WORSHIPPING HER INVOKES BRAVERY, SELF-CONFIDENCE, AND PROTECTION.

COLOR: WHITE

BRAVERY BADGES

DESIGN A BRAVERY BADGE OR A SYMBOL OF COURAGE, JUST LIKE KATYAYANI MAA'S FEARLESSNESS IN THE FACE OF DANGER

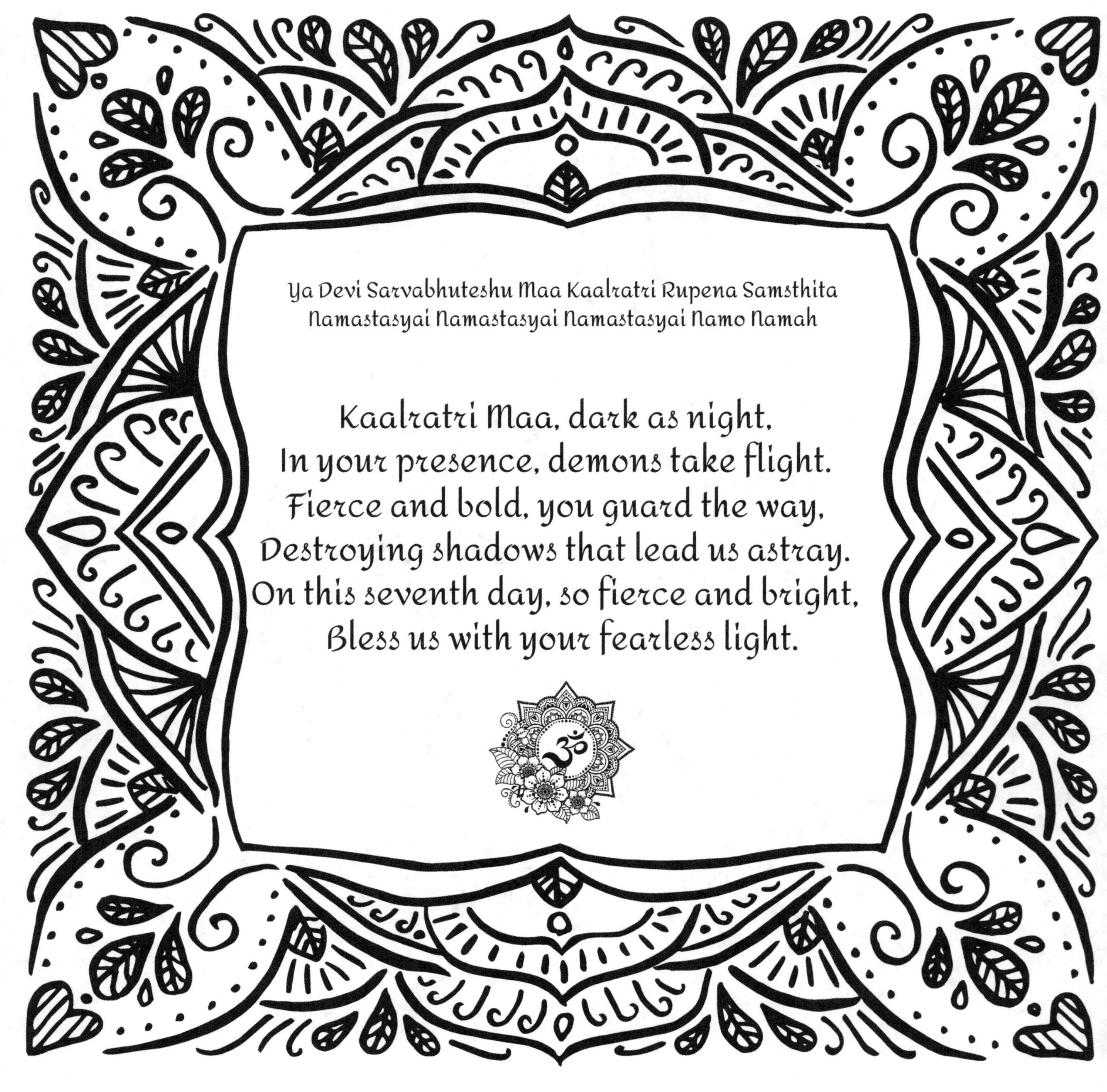

Ya Devi Sarvabhuteshu Maa Kaalratri Rupena Samsthita
Namastasyai Namastasyai Namastasyai Namo Namah

Kaalratri Maa, dark as night,
In your presence, demons take flight.
Fierce and bold, you guard the way,
Destroying shadows that lead us astray.
On this seventh day, so fierce and bright,
Bless us with your fearless light.

Kaalratri Maa

KALARATRI MAA

THE GODDESS OF DESTRUCTION

SYMBOLISM: KALARATRI MAA IS THE MOST FEROCIOUS AND TERRIFYING FORM OF DURGA. SHE REPRESENTS THE DESTRUCTION OF IGNORANCE AND DARKNESS, PURGING EVIL FORCES AND LIBERATING SOULS.

ICONOGRAPHY: SHE IS DEPICTED WITH A DARK COMPLEXION, DISHEVELED HAIR, AND A TERRIFYING FACE. SHE RIDES A DONKEY AND HOLDS A SWORD AND A TRIDENT, SYMBOLIZING THE DESTRUCTION OF NEGATIVE FORCES. FLAMES SHOOT FROM HER NOSTRILS, AND HER PRESENCE STRIKES FEAR INTO DEMONS, SIGNIFYING HER ROLE AS THE GODDESS WHO ERADICATES FEAR AND EVIL.

SIGNIFICANCE: KALARATRI MAA DESTROYS IGNORANCE AND DARKNESS. DEVOTEES SEEK HER PROTECTION TO RID THEMSELVES OF FEAR, IGNORANCE, AND EVIL FORCES. SHE SIGNIFIES THE REMOVAL OF OBSTACLES AND THE DAWN OF ENLIGHTENMENT.

COLOR: BLACK

AUSPICIOUS WEAPONS

DRAW THE AUSPICIOUS WEAPONS IN KALARATRI MAA'S HANDS

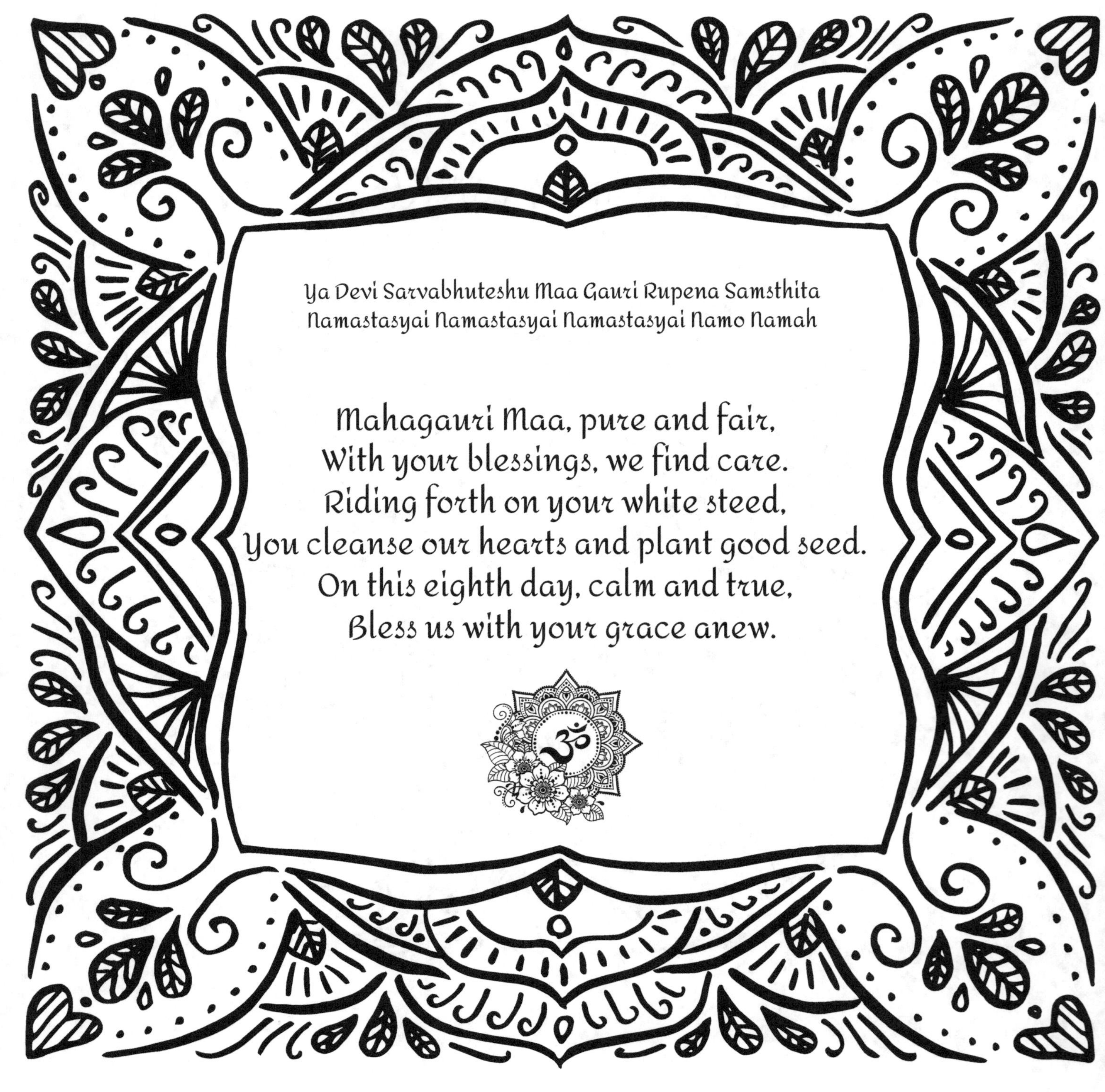

Ya Devi Sarvabhuteshu Maa Gauri Rupena Samsthita
Namastasyai Namastasyai Namastasyai Namo Namah

Mahagauri Maa, pure and fair,
With your blessings, we find care.
Riding forth on your white steed,
You cleanse our hearts and plant good seed.
On this eighth day, calm and true,
Bless us with your grace anew.

Mahagauri Maa

MAHAGAURI MAA

THE GODDESS OF PURITY AND PEACE

SYMBOLISM: MAHAGAURI MAA REPRESENTS PURITY, CALMNESS, AND SERENITY. SHE IS WORSHIPPED FOR HER ABILITY TO PURIFY THE SOUL, REMOVE SINS, AND GRANT BLESSINGS OF WISDOM AND CLARITY.

ICONOGRAPHY: MAHAGAURI MAA IS SEEN RIDING A WHITE BULL, SYMBOLIZING PURITY AND SIMPLICITY. SHE HAS FOUR ARMS, WITH ONE HOLDING A TRIDENT AND ANOTHER A DAMARU (SMALL DRUM). HER FAIR COMPLEXION SHINES LIKE A PEARL, REPRESENTING PURITY AND SPIRITUAL BEAUTY.

SIGNIFICANCE: WORSHIPPING MAHAGAURI MAA BRINGS PEACE, SERENITY, AND THE REMOVAL OF SUFFERING. SHE REPRESENTS THE ULTIMATE FORM OF COMPASSION AND TRANQUILITY, GUIDING HER DEVOTEES TOWARDS ENLIGHTENMENT AND CONTENTMENT.

COLOR: YELLOW

COLOR THE LOTUS

COLOR THE LOTUS FLOWER REPRESENTING MAHAGAURI'S PURITY

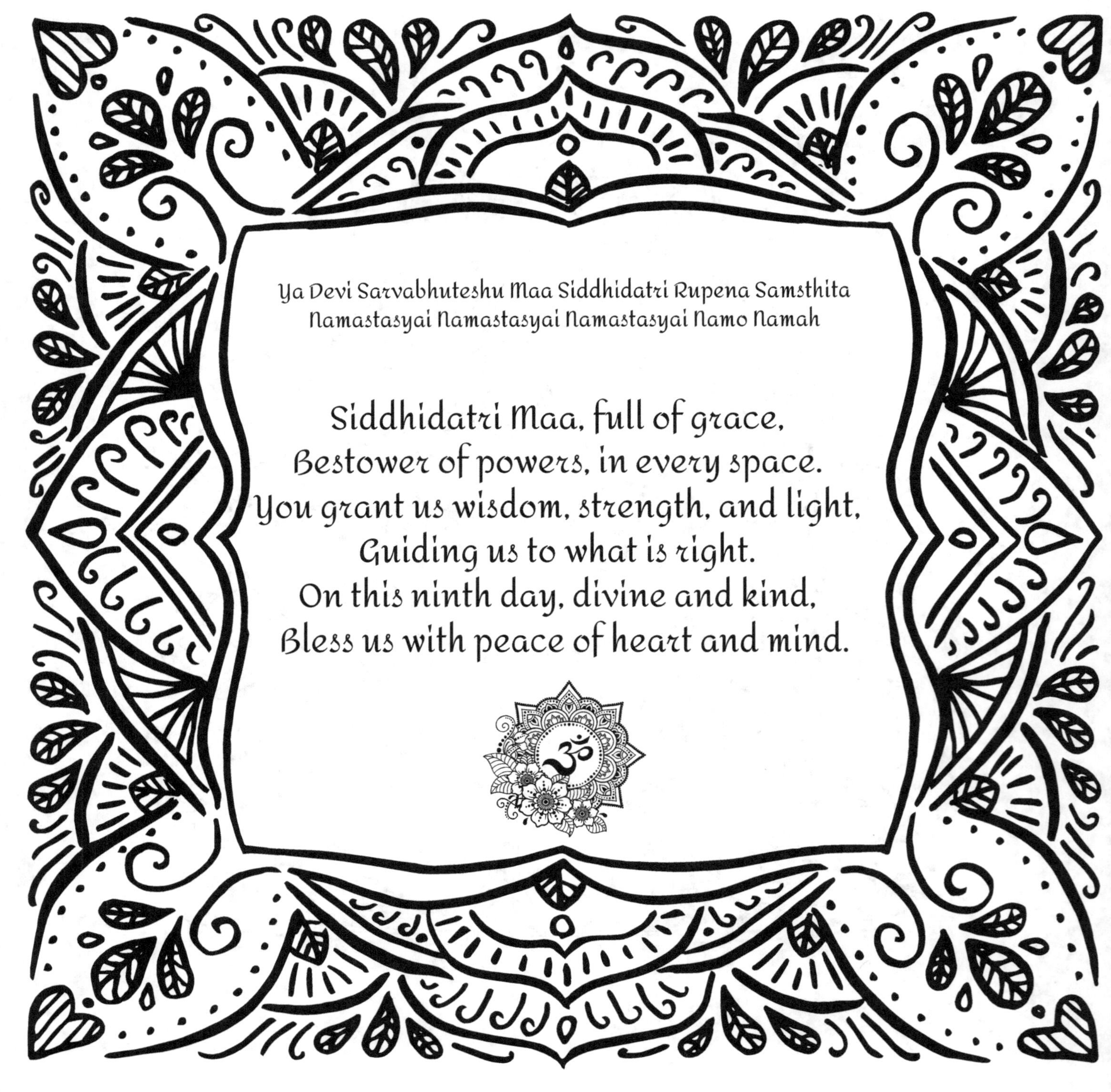

Ya Devi Sarvabhuteshu Maa Siddhidatri Rupena Samsthita
Namastasyai Namastasyai Namastasyai Namo Namah

Siddhidatri Maa, full of grace,
Bestower of powers, in every space.
You grant us wisdom, strength, and light,
Guiding us to what is right.
On this ninth day, divine and kind,
Bless us with peace of heart and mind.

Siddhidatri Maa

SIDDHIDATRI MAA
THE GIVER OF ULTIMATE KNOWLEDGE

SYMBOLISM: SIDDHIDATRI MAA IS THE GODDESS OF SUPERNATURAL POWERS (SIDDHIS). SHE SYMBOLIZES THE ULTIMATE REALIZATION OF DIVINE ENERGY AND IS WORSHIPPED AS THE GIVER OF ACCOMPLISHMENTS AND FULFILLMENT.

ICONOGRAPHY: SHE IS DEPICTED SEATED ON A LOTUS OR A LION, HOLDING A CHAKRA, MACE, CONCH, AND LOTUS IN HER HANDS. SURROUNDED BY CELESTIAL BEINGS, HER CALM AND BENEVOLENT FACE REFLECTS HER POWER TO BESTOW DIVINE WISDOM AND SPIRITUAL KNOWLEDGE.

SIGNIFICANCE: SIDDHIDATRI MAA BLESSES HER DEVOTEES WITH MYSTICAL POWERS AND SPIRITUAL REALIZATION. SHE REPRESENTS THE FULFILLMENT OF SPIRITUAL DESIRES AND THE ATTAINMENT OF HIGHER KNOWLEDGE, REMINDING US OF THE VAST POTENTIAL WITHIN EACH SOUL TO ACHIEVE THE DIVINE.

COLOR: RED

GRANT A WISH

WRITE OR DRAW A WISH YOU WOULD ASK SIDDHIDATRI MAA TO GRANT

www.ingramcontent.com/pod-product-compliance
Lightning Source LLC
Chambersburg PA
CBHW080602300726

48975CB00010B/2768